We dedicate this book to him!

And also to Rik Mayall,
who was our hero.

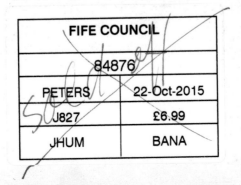

Contents

Introduction

We all love Christmas! He loves it, she loves it, they all love it . . . But a while ago we got a phone call from that chubby fella Father Christmas, and he explained that he'd lost two of his 'ho's'. All he could say was: 'Ho!' Without his laugh, how would people know he was the real Father Christmas? They might think he was just one of those pretend ones that work in shops and make small children cry. So he asked us to write a very funny Christmas joke book, so that his 'Ho, ho, ho!' would return.

We visited the North Pole and had a two-week party with the elves in their local gaff, where we came up with the inspiration for this book.

What you will find inside this book are quality jokes and other bits from Father Christmas's special 'funny' sack which will make your usual cracker jokes seem about as funny as Mrs Christmas's hanky.

It's nuts, it's stuffed and if you don't like it, wrap it in bacon and shove it inside the turkey!

Happy Christmas, you bunch of turkey basters!

Why does
Santa have
three gardens?
*So he can
'ho-ho-ho!'*

What's furry
and minty?
A polo bear

2

What does Santa do with fat elves?
He sends them to an elf farm

Dick and Dom's
TWELVE DAYS OF CHRISTMAS

On the first day of Christmas my
Dickie gave to me . . . a fat trout
in me mum's tea

What says, 'Oh, oh, oh!'?
Santa walking backwards

What do Santa's little helpers learn at school?
The elf-abet

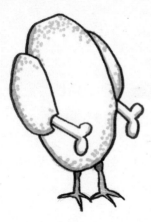

Where does Santa go
when he's sick?
To the elf centre

Where do elves go to dance?
Christmas balls!

6

What's worse than Rudolph
with a runny nose?
*Frosty the snowman with a
hot flush*

Dick and Dom's
Top Five
Uses for a Dead Christmas Tree

1) Cut it up into small pieces, put it in a bag and give it to some wrinklies as an exciting 3D jigsaw puzzle

2) Swap it for one of 'those two' off *The One Show*

3) Dress it up as your nana and
drop it in a puddle

4) Put it in a bap and sneeze all over it

5) Hang sausages on it and send it to
Blue Peter (they'll love it!)

To: Blue Peter,
BBC Place,
Wherever.

Why did the turkey cross the road?
Because it was the chicken's day off

What happened to the turkey at Christmas?
It got gobbled!

What is the best
Christmas present
in the world?
*A broken drum –
you just can't beat it*

How does Good King
Wenceslas like his pizza?
Deep-pan, crisp and even

A Letter to Father Christmas

Dear Father Christmas,

I have been a very good boy this year . . . apart from blocking the toilet, pushing my brother over, putting jam on the cat, 'accidentally' throwing a full dog-poo bag into Mr Johnson's garden, smearing fish paste on the doorknobs, shoving sausages up the car exhaust pipe, shaving Dad's head while he was asleep and locking my nana in the cupboard under the stairs like the one that Harry Potter lives in, but without the magic or luxury or owls.

Will any of the above information affect how many presents I get?

Please reply quickly – my dinner's ready in five minutes.

Jimmy

Who hides in
the bakery at
Christmas?
A mince spy

What happened to
the man who stole an
Advent calendar?
He got twenty-five days!

Dick: What do crackers, fruitcake and nuts remind you of?
Dom: *You!*

Knock, knock!
Who's there?
Hanna.
Hanna who?
Hanna partridge in a pear tree.

What did the
beaver say to the
Christmas tree?
'Nice gnawing you.'

Dom: Doctor, doctor, I seem to have a mince pie stuck up my bottom.
Doctor: *Well, you're in luck because I've got just the cream for that.*

What's Behind the Advent-calendar Door?

A fat bloke pouring brandy butter all over his head

How can Santa's sleigh possibly
fly through the air?
*You would too if you were
pulled by flying reindeer*

How do you make a
slow reindeer fast?
Don't feed it!

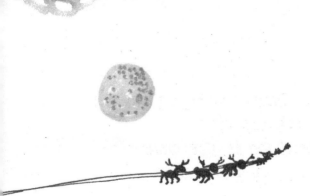

And as the reindeer
say before they tell you
jokes . . .
*'These jokes will sleigh
you!'*

Finish It Off

Finish this drawing of Santa and his Spam
pram and colour it in!

How does Rudolph know
when Christmas is coming?
He looks at his calen-deer!

How do you get into
Donner's house?
You ring the deer-bell!

How would you get four reindeer in a car?
Two in the front and two in the back

And how do you get four polar bears in a car?
Take the reindeer out first

22

What goes
'Ho! Ho! Ho! Thump!'?
*Father Christmas
laughing his head off!*

What did Cinderella say
when the chemist lost
her photographs?
*'Some day my prints
will come.'*

What's
a ghost's
favourite
Christmas
entertainment?
A phantomime!

What did the mum
turkey say to her
naughty chicks?
*'If your father could see
you he would roll over
in his grave-y.'*

What's Behind the Advent-calendar Door?

A lollipop lady licking her festive lollipop

Dick and Dom's
TWELVE DAYS OF CHRISTMAS

On the second day of Christmas my
Dickie gave to me . . . two turtles' heads
and a fat trout in me mum's tea

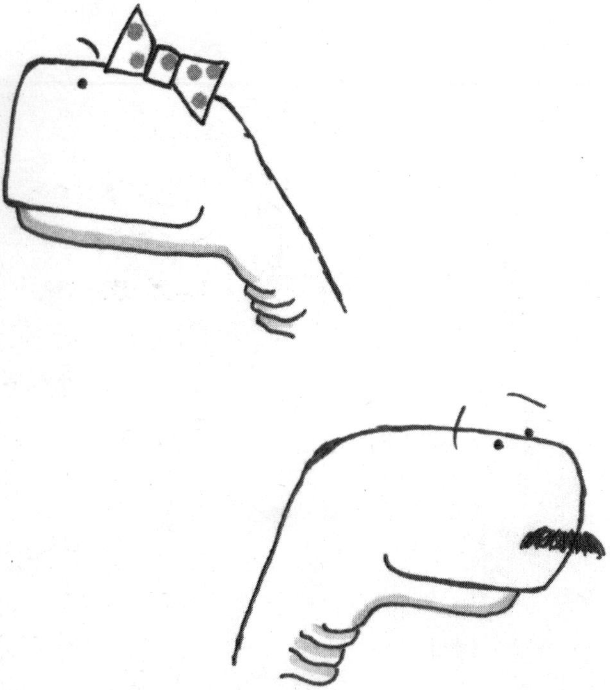

I'm so strong I could lift a reindeer with one hand.
Yeah, but where are we going to find a one-handed reindeer?

What's the scariest pantomime?
Ghouldilocks and the Three Bears

What does Father
Christmas do
when his elves
misbehave?
*He gives them
the sack*

How do elves greet
each other?
'Small world, isn't it?'

How do you
describe a
rich elf?
Welfy

Festive
BOREDOM BUSTERS

Make Your Own Father Christmas Outfit

1) Take out some very expensive
   clothes and paint them red. Let
   them dry and then put them on

2) Shave a rabbit* and
   stick its fur to your
   face using honey

HONEY

3) Run down the street screaming

4) Go home, sit down
   and think about what
   you've done

*A toy rabbit! Who would
shave a real rabbit?
I mean, *really*?

31

How many elves does it take to change a light bulb? *Ten! One to change the light bulb and nine to stand on the others' shoulders*

What do you call
a kid who doesn't
believe in Santa?
*A rebel without a
Claus!*

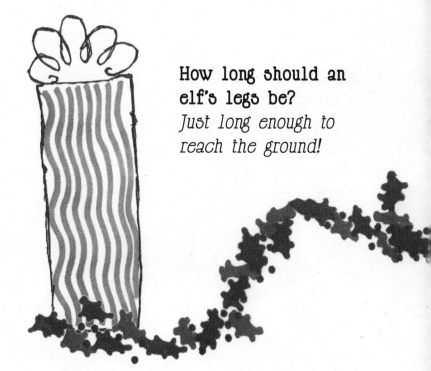

How long should an
elf's legs be?
*Just long enough to
reach the ground!*

If athletes get athlete's foot, what do elves get?
Mistle-toes

Why do seals swim in salt water?
Because pepper water makes them sneeze

What's Behind the Advent-calendar Door?

Eamonn Holmes dressed as a fairy

DICK AND DOM'S CHRISTMAS STUFF
WITH NUTS AND STUFFING

Scrooge's favourite jacket-potato filling is Bob Cratchit's mango-chutney sorbet

Christmas pudding was invented by Elton John's brother, John John

Rudolph's real name is Darren and he is wanted by the police

One in every million Christmas Crackers contains a human pop tart

Turkey is just a big fat ugly chicken

Why couldn't the Christmas tree stand up?
Because it didn't have any legs

What do snowmen eat for breakfast?
Snowflakes

Which of Santa's reindeer has the worst manners?

Rude-olph

Where does a snowman keep his money?
In a snow bank

How much did Santa pay for his sleigh?
Nothing, it was on the house!

Why is Santa so good
at karate?
*Because he has a
black belt*

What do you call a
snowman in the summer?
A puddle

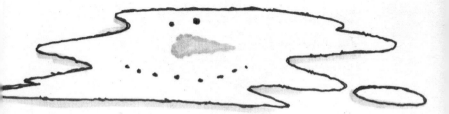

41

Finish It Off

Finish this drawing of a monkey-man wearing a Santa hat, standing on a wiggy pig!

What kind of bug
hates Christmas?
A humbug

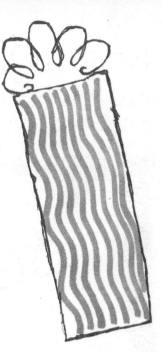

What did the
reindeer say when
he saw an elf?
*Nothing, reindeer
can't talk*

A wonderful
Christmas song told
me to 'Deck the
Halls' . . .
so I did.
*Mr and Mrs Hall
were not very happy*

If there were eleven
elves, and another one
came along, what would
he be?
The tw-elf

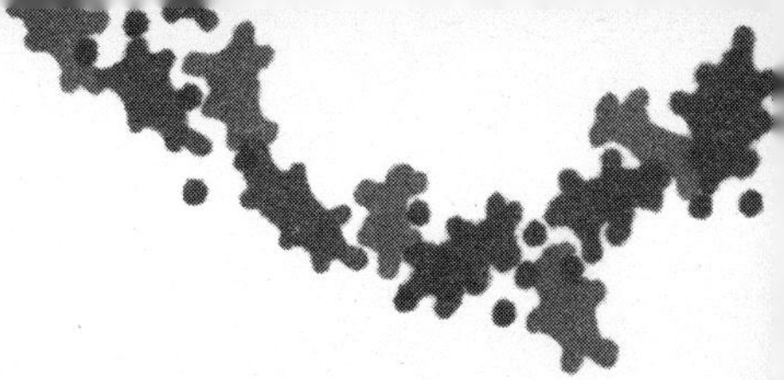

Santa rides in a
sleigh. What do
elves ride in?
Minivans

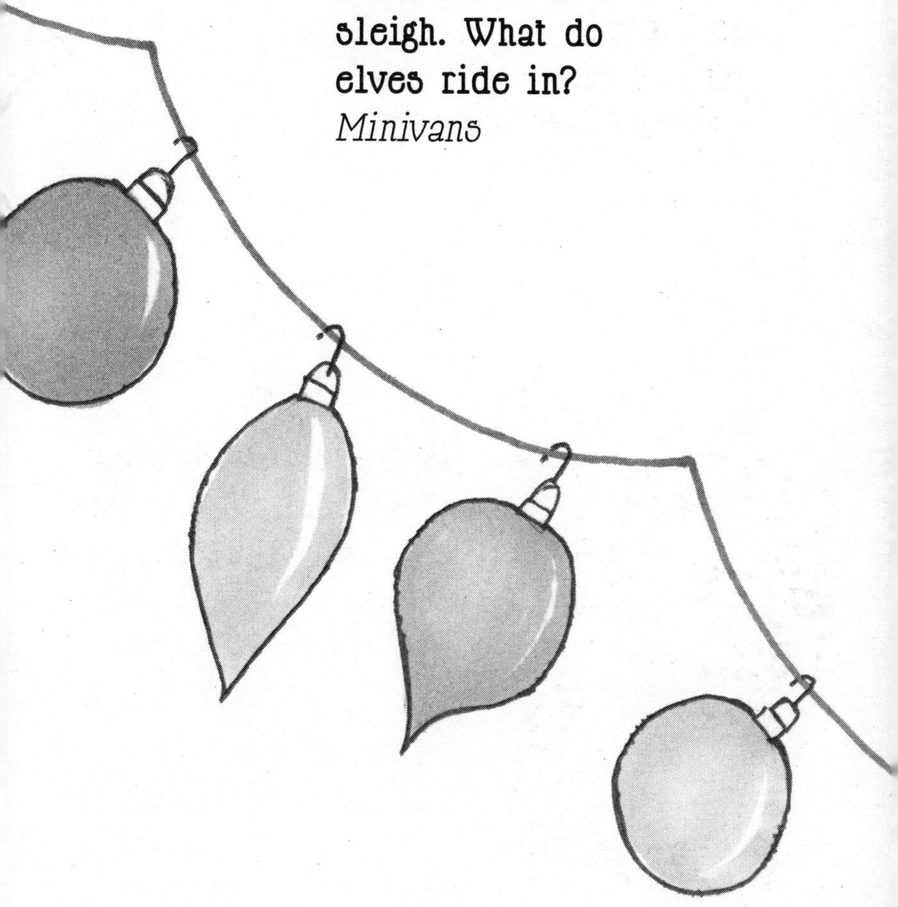

Never catch snowflakes on your tongue until all the birds have gone south for the winter!

What do you call an elf wearing earmuffs? *Anything you want. He can't hear you!*

What's Behind the Advent-calendar Door?

An
invisible
snowman
vomiting

STOP ... CAROL TIME

Fill in the blanks to make up new versions of famous carols using the list of words below.

SNOB-HONKERS

RAGING SNOBS

SNOB-BISCUITS

SNOBLETS

SNOB-OMELETTE

SNOB-BANDIT

SNOB

When Santa got stuck up the _____,

He began to _____.

You girls and _____ won't get any

_____

If you don't pull me out.

My beard is black, there's soot in my

_____,

My nose is _____ too.

When Santa got stuck up the _____,

Aaachooo, achoo, achoo.

49

What did the little
elves have to do
when they got home
from school?
Gnome-work!

What do you call
a smelly Santa?
Farter Christmas

What do you call Father
Christmas's cat on the beach?
Sandy Claus

What does an
electrician get
for Christmas?
Shorts

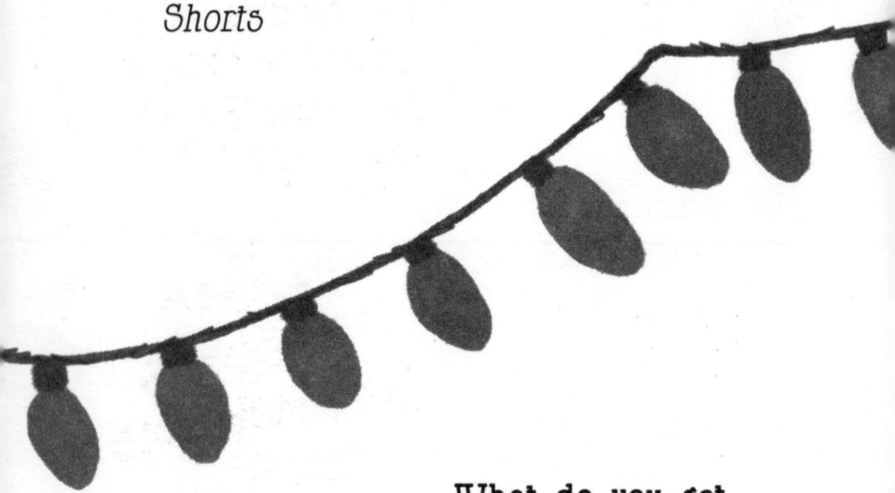

What do you get
when you cross an
archer with a
gift-wrapper?
Ribbon Hood

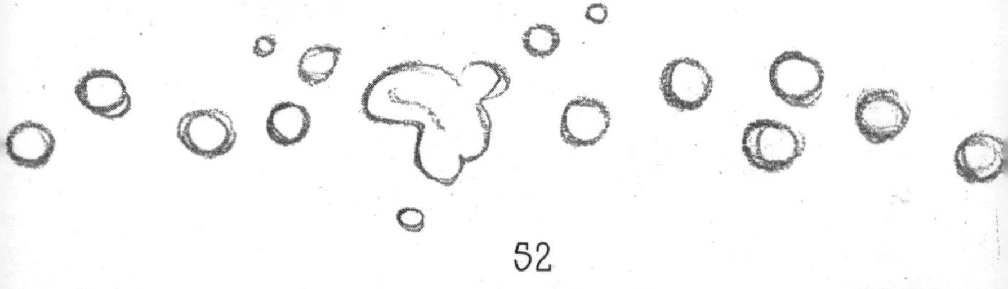

Two snowmen are standing in a field. One says to the other, 'Do you smell carrots?'

Be naughty – save Santa the trip.

Christmas Wordsearch 1

Words run down and left to right.

BISCUIT
BOGIES
BUM
CRACKER
CUSTARD
DRUM
FART
FATHER CHRISTMAS
GOBBLED
HANKY
HAT
HO HO HO
JELLY

KNICKERS
LITTLE HELPER
NORTH POLE
PENGUIN
POLAR BORE
POO
RED
REINDEER
SANTA
SILLY
STOCKING
TURKEY
UNDER

F	A	R	T	C	D	D	Q	B	P	F	B	R	W	B
A	D	C	V	U	U	G	A	S	O	Q	X	E	X	O
T	Z	B	N	S	J	O	S	T	O	C	K	I	N	G
H	W	N	V	T	H	B	U	U	K	R	P	N	J	I
E	P	O	L	A	R	B	O	R	E	A	E	D	E	E
R	C	R	U	R	Y	L	N	K	K	C	N	E	F	S
C	D	T	S	D	T	E	M	E	S	K	G	E	N	G
H	O	H	O	H	O	D	H	Y	G	E	U	R	E	D
R	F	P	K	A	X	N	G	E	Y	R	I	H	M	R
I	R	O	S	N	S	B	D	R	H	B	N	F	F	U
S	K	L	T	K	N	I	C	K	E	R	S	B	U	M
T	H	E	X	Y	O	S	S	T	S	E	I	A	N	N
M	S	K	H	J	U	C	E	J	E	L	L	Y	D	S
A	Y	T	A	K	L	U	F	Y	F	A	L	H	E	H
S	A	N	T	A	A	I	Y	J	Q	D	Y	D	R	M
E	J	B	L	I	T	T	L	E	H	E	L	P	E	R

Why did the elf
push his bed into
the fireplace?
*He wanted to sleep
like a log*

Who sings 'White
Christmas' and then
explodes?
Bang Crosby

What's red and
white and goes up
and down?
*Father Christmas
stuck in a lift*

Where do
snowmen
dance?
Snowballs

What goes, 'Now you see
me, now you don't, now you
see me, now you don't'?
*A snowflake blowing over a
zebra crossing*

What's Behind the Advent-calendar Door?

A thin Christmas monkey

A Letter to Father Christmas

Dear Santa,

I have not been a good boy this year, mainly because I'm a girl.

This year I'm not going to leave anything out for you. I think that this will speed up your mission on Christmas Eve and help you lead a healthier lifestyle. The carrot that I normally leave out for your reindeer I have donated to the charity shop and the glass of milk I have given to a local donkey called Geoff. Please still bring me presents and stuff, but don't expect any snacks or juice or whatever.

Merry Christmas anyway,

Jasmine

What did Mrs Claus
say to Santa Claus?
'It looks like rain, dear!'

Who is never hungry at Christmas?
The turkey – it's always stuffed

Dick and Dom's
TWELVE DAYS OF CHRISTMAS

On the third day of Christmas my
Dickie gave to me . . . three French
pigs, two turtles' heads and a fat trout
in me mum's tea

What do you call a
reindeer with no eyes?
No eye deer

What do you call
a reindeer with
no eyes and no
legs?
Still no eye deer

Why did the
reindeer cross
the road?
*Because he was
tied to a chicken*

Knock, knock!
Who's there?
Wayne.
Wayne who?
Our Wayne in
a manger!

What do you
call people who
are scared of
Christmas?
Claus-trophobic

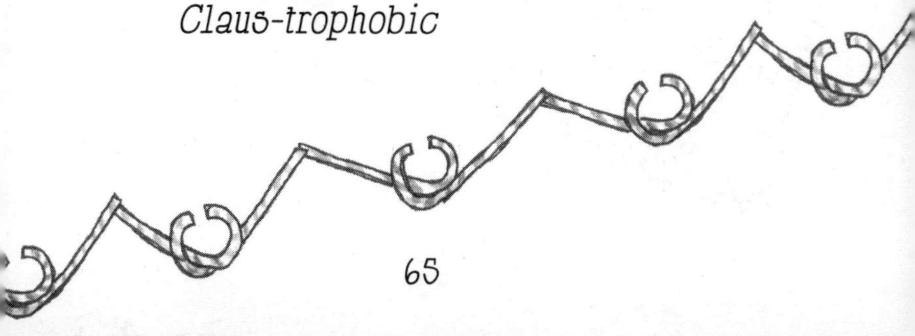

DICK AND DOM'S CHRISTMAS STUFF
WITH NUTS AND STUFFING

Elves have no sense of humour as they are too busy wiping dribble off toys

Father Christmas's wife once appeared on *Tipping Point*

Every time you pinch a chocolate decoration off the Christmas tree a duck's beak falls off

In prehistoric times cavemen used to lick each other like lollipops under the mistletoe

Stuffing doesn't have a proper name as it is simply made from 'stuff' and 'ing'

Dom: Doctor, doctor, I keep stealing things when I go Christmas shopping.

Doctor: *Try this medicine . . . and if it doesn't work come back and bring me a new video camera.*

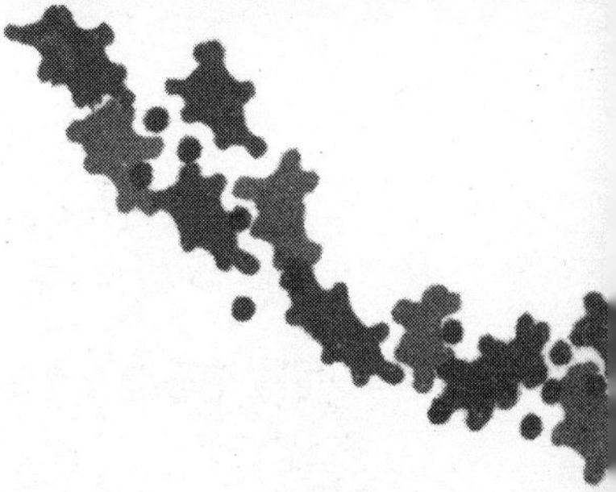

A Christmas
thought:
*STRESSED is just
DESSERTS spelled
backwards*

How long does it
take to burn an
Advent candle
down?
About a wick

Dick and Dom's
Top Five
Presents for Your Parents

1) Broccoli stalks

2) A chimp on a stick

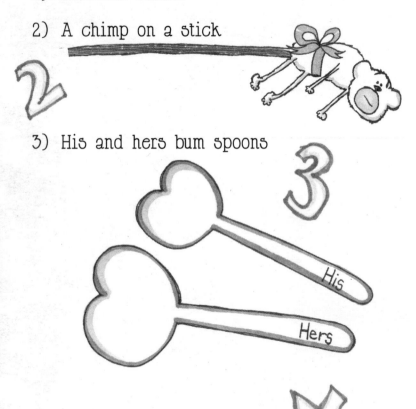

3) His and hers bum spoons

4) Susan Boyle's boiled boils

5) Ant and Dec's trophy-wiping hanky

What's
Behind the
Advent-
calendar
Door?

McBusted's
special
Christmas
double
whoopee-
whopper

Dick: Doctor, doctor, I keep thinking I'm a Christmas bell! **Doctor:** *Just take these pills – and if they don't work, give me a ring.*

REMEMBER.
A bell is for life,
Not just for Christmas.
Thank you.

What do you call
a reindeer with
cotton wool in
his ears?
Anything you like,
he can't hear you!

One snowy night Father Christmas was checking the sledge, switching all the lights on to make sure that they were working.

Father Christmas: Are my indicators working, Elf Dick?
Elf Dick: *Yes – no – yes – no – yes – no – yes – no . . .*

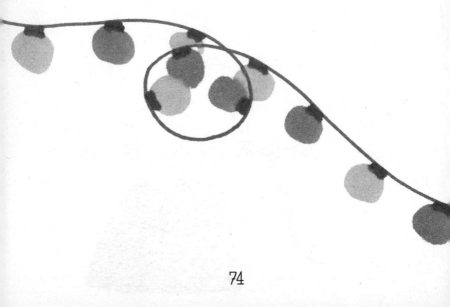

What do you get
hanging from Father
Christmas's roof?
Tired arms

What's a hairdresser's
favourite Christmas carol?
'O Comb, All Ye Faithful'

Dom: Doctor, doctor, with all the excitement of Christmas I just can't sleep!
Doctor: *Try lying on the edge of your bed – you'll soon drop off.*

Why does Father Christmas cry a lot?
Because he gets a little santamental!

Dick: What has antlers, pulls Father Christmas's sleigh and is made of cement?
Dom: *I don't know.*
Dick: A reindeer!
Dom: *What about the cement?*
Dick: I just threw that in to make it hard!

How do elves take
self-portraits on their
mobile phones?
With an elfie-stick

Dick: Did you hear
about the time that
Father Christmas lost
his underpants . . .
Dom: *That's how he
became known as Saint
Knickerless!*

Knock, knock!
Who's there?
Snow.
Snow who?
Snowbody!

Festive BOREDOM BUSTERS

Family Christmas Game Time

1) Gather the family around the table

2) Number the family from one to six*

3) Roll a fat dice

4) Whichever person's number it lands on, push that person off their chair

5) When everyone is on the floor sprinkle them with glitter

6) Tell them if anyone moves before New Year's Day, Santa's snot goblin will get them

*If you haven't got six family members, invite the local vicar and his mates

BUSTED!

81

What's Behind the Advent-calendar Door?

A Christmas lifeboat

Father Christmas: Doctor, doctor, can you do anything about my bald patch?

Doctor: *I have some good news and some bad news. The bad news is I can't make hair grow . . . but the good news is I can shrink your head so the little bit of hair you've still got fits.*

What do you get if you cross a turkey with a harp?
A turkey that can pluck itself

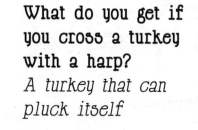

Father Christmas: Elf Dom, I thought I told you to go out there and clear the snow!
Elf Dom: *I'm on my way, Father Christmas!*
Father Christmas: But you've only got one welly on.
Elf Dom: *That's all right. There's only one foot of snow.*

What sort of mobile phone has Santa got?
Pay as you ho, ho, ho!

What do you get
if you cross Santa
with a flying
saucer?
A UF-ho, ho, ho!

What do you get
if you cross Santa
with a gardener?
*Someone who likes
to hoe, hoe, hoe!*

Finish It Off

Finish this drawing of a grumpy granny elf trying to stuff a surprised-looking turkey!

Dick and Dom's
TWELVE DAYS OF CHRISTMAS

On the fourth day of Christmas
my Dickie gave to me . . . four
pregnant men, three French
pigs, two turtles' heads and
a fat trout in me mum's tea

Christmas Crossword 1

Across

2) A pantomime cat in shoes, Puss in _ _ _ _ _ (5)

5) A reindeer with a red nose (7)

8) One third of Father Christmas's famous laugh (2)

9) The opposite of 'yuck' (3)

10) The Ghost of Christmas _ _ _ _ (4)

11) After Christmas Eve comes Christmas _ _ _ (3)

12) A pudding made of pastry and filled with mince can only be a mince _ _ _ (3)

14) These animals pull the Christmas sleigh (8)

15) The correct response to: 'Have you been good this year?' (3)

Down

1) Many people have this bird roasted for Christmas lunch (6)

3) These veggies will make your bot-bot do smelly parps (7)

4) A little person, often dressed in green, who works in Santa's workshop (3)

6) Most rock bands have one of these, but a turkey has two (8)
7) Another word for 'merry', often used before the words 'New Year' (5)
13) The colour of Father Christmas's work uniform (3)

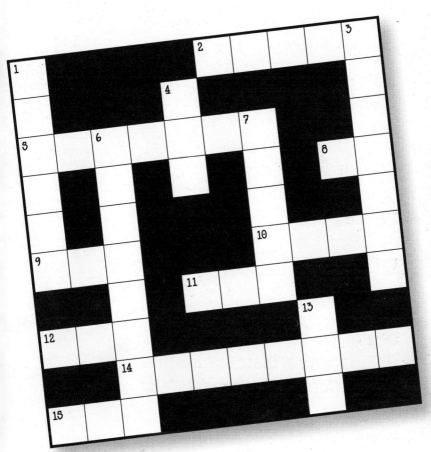

See page 289 for answers

What does Father Christmas write on his
Christmas cards?
ABCDEFGHIJKMNOPQRSTUVWXYZ (No-L!)

Dear Mrs Christmas,
ABCDEFGHIJKMNOPQRSTUVWXYZ.
Love from
Father Christmas
x x x

What do ducks do
before their
Christmas dinner?
*Pull their Christmas
quackers!*

Knock, knock!
Who's there?
Avery.
Avery who?
Avery merry Christmas!

Knock, knock!
Who's there?
Police.
Police who?
Police don't make
me eat all my
Brussels sprouts!

Dick: Can I have a dog for
Christmas?
Dom: *No, you can have turkey
like everyone else!*

92

Dom: Will the Christmas pudding be long?
Dick: *No, silly, it'll be round!*

What's Behind the Advent-calendar Door?

An ant nativity

Dick and Dom's
Top Five

Things to Say While Eating Sprouts

1) 'These taste like my farts smell!'

2) 'It all seems like fun now, but you'll be sorry later!'

3) 'Uncle Booboo make go away!'

4) 'These look like Yoda's gobstoppers'

5) Cry loudly

How do you drain
your Christmas
Brussels sprouts?
*With an Advent
colander*

Why do bees
hum carols?
*Because they've
forgotten the words!*

Knock, knock!
Who's there?
Wanda.
Wanda who?
Wanda know what you're getting for Christmas?

Hi I'm Wanda KnowwhatyouregettingforChristmas. Crazy surname, I know, but look at my giant hands! Perfect for squeezing presents and gifts so I know what you're getting for Christmas. Yessir! Yeehaw!

STOP . . . CAROL TIME

Fill in the blanks to make up new versions of famous carols using the list of words below.

BUM-MUFFIN

TURKEY PIPES

JEREMY PIMPLE

HAM-TOOT

STINKING BISHOP

FAT KNEES

BABBA

Little donkey, little _____,

On the _____ road,

Got to keep on plodding onwards

With your precious _____.

Been a long time, little _____,

Through the _____ night.

Don't give up now, little _____,

_____ in sight.

What is an ig?

An igloo without a toilet

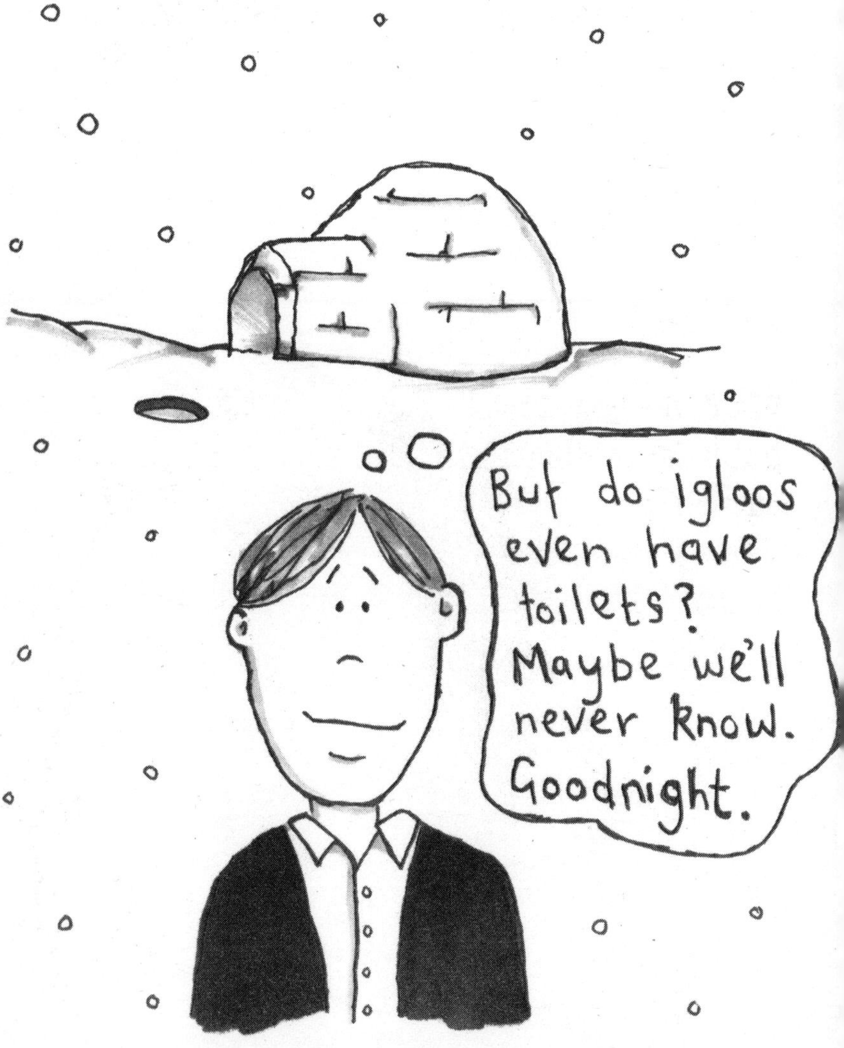

What do elephants sing at Christmas?
'No-el(ephants), no-el(ephants)!'

What do you call a polar bear wearing earmuffs?
Whatever you want – he can't hear you!

Why is it so cold
at Christmas?
*Because it's
Decembrrrrr*

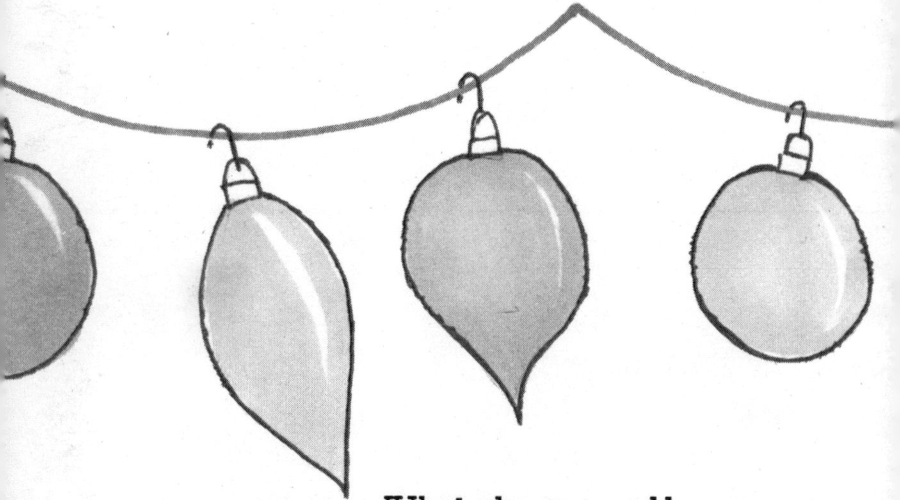

What do you call a man
wrapped in Christmas
wrapping paper?
Russell

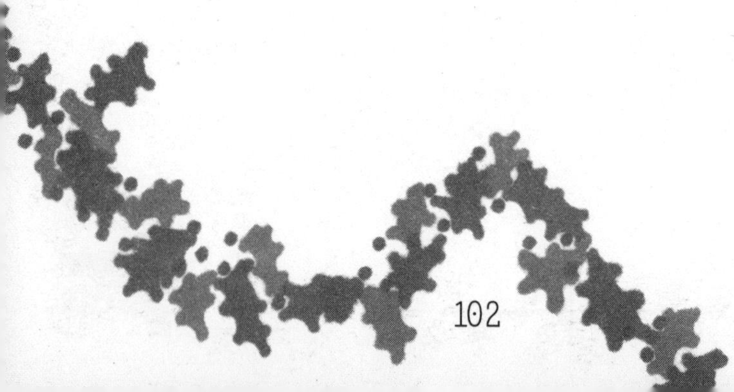

Dick and Dom's
TWELVE DAYS OF CHRISTMAS

On the fifth day of Christmas my
Dickie gave to me . . . five cold things,
four pregnant men, three French pigs,
two turtles' heads and a fat trout in me
mum's tea

Frozen
Peas

Antarctica

What's
Behind the
Advent-
calendar
Door?

Jamie Oliver's
tongue in a
Christmas
stocking

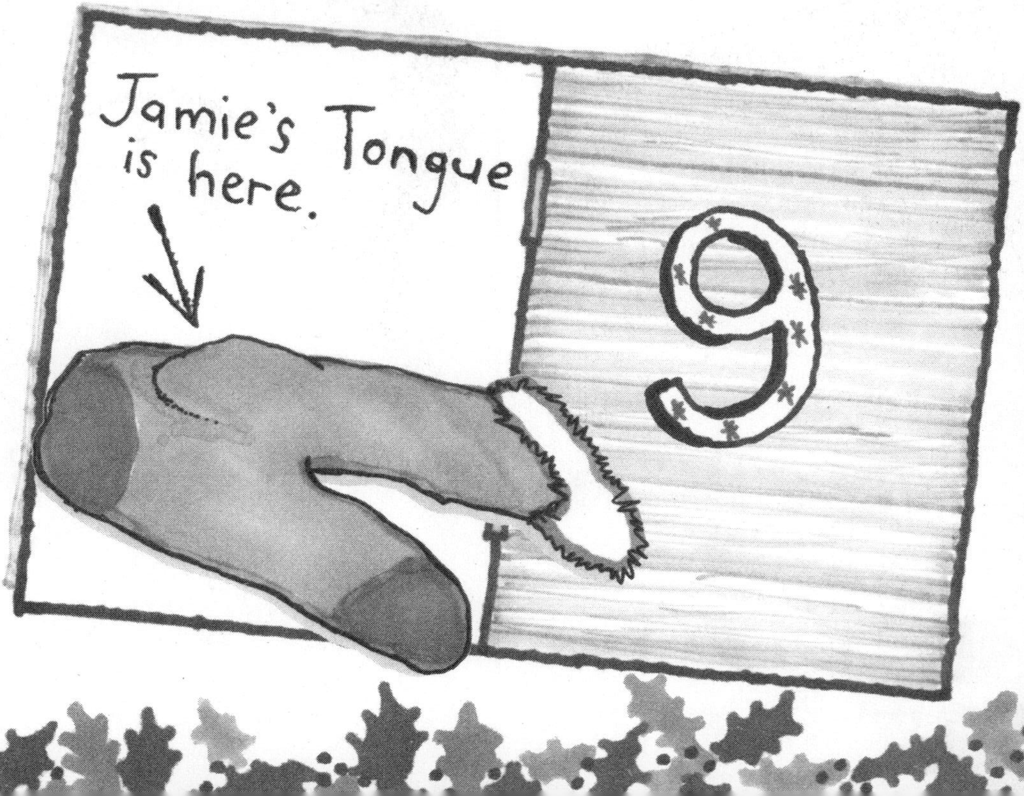

What do snow
children have for
breakfast?
Ice Krispies

What did one snowman
say to the other?
'Ice to see you!'

What's Father
Christmas's
favourite food?
*Stir-fried ice and
chilly sauce*

What did Adam
say the day before
Christmas?
It's Christmas, Eve!

What do you get if you cross an ant with a reindeer?
Antlers

Hi, I'm Pretend Pharrell Williams, here to wish you a Happy Christmas, Happy New Year, Happy Birthday, Happy Car Wash, Happy HAPPY HAPPY HAPPY HAPPY HAPPY

What do you tell a
stressed snowman?
Chill out, man!

What do snowmen wear on their heads?
Ice caps

A Letter to Father Christmas

DEAR BIG MAN,

FOR MY CHRISTMAS I DON'T WANT ANYTHING EXCEPT A NEW MUM AND DAD. YOU SEE, MINE WEAR SOCKS WITH CROCS, WHICH MAKES ME FEEL SICK. THEY ALSO GENERALLY GET ON MY NERVES.

IF YOU COULD POSSIBLY REPLACE THEM WITH COOL PEOPLE, LIKE A HOLLYWOOD STAR OR A MEMBER OF AN AWESOME BAND, THAT'D BE MINT.

MY MUM COULD EASILY BE RECYCLED BY OFFERING HER TO BE A MUM TO SOMEBODY ELSE, BUT MY DAD IS GENUINELY USELESS AND IS ONLY GOOD TO USE AS A GOALPOST OR MAYBE A SCARECROW.

YEAH, THANKS AND ALL THAT,

RICKY (LITTLE MAN)

What's Behind the Advent-calendar Door?

Captain Chapatti

What's a snowman's
favourite
Mexican food?
Brrrr-itos

How do you know
that Santa is a
good racing driver?
*He's always in
pole position*

What do witches use
to wrap their Christmas
presents?
Spell-o-tape

What did the farmer
get for Christmas?
A cow-culator

What do you call
a man who claps
at Christmas?
Santa-pplause

Christmas Join the Dots 1

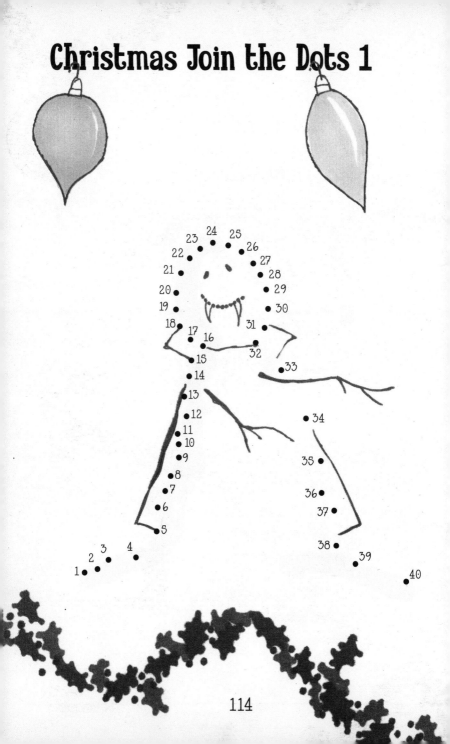

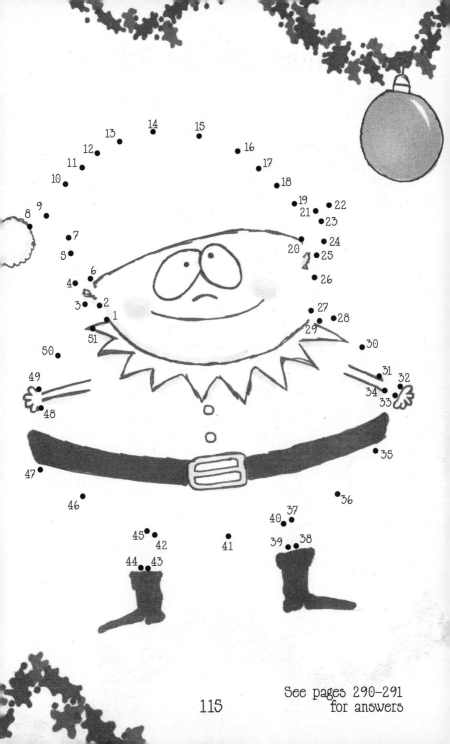

115

See pages 290-291
for answers

What do you get if you
cross Father Christmas
with a detective?
Santa Clues

What do you
say when Father
Christmas is taking
the register?
Present

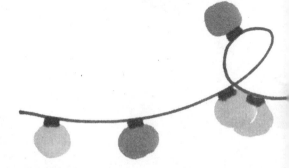

What smells most in a chimney?
Santa's nose

What's fat and jolly
and runs on eight
wheels?
*Father Christmas
on roller skates*

What's red and white
and red and white and
red and white?
*Father Christmas rolling
down a hill*

Why did Rudolph
wear sunglasses to the
beach?
*Because he didn't want
to be recognized*

Turkey Piñata

1. Put some dead batteries and a note saying 'Toy Not Included' into Stephen Mulhern's limited edition 'smelly bag'

2. Insert the smelly bag into a turkey carcass

3. Using string, dangle the carcass from the ceiling and give the family baseball bats

4. Make your family smack the turkey with the bats until the smelly bag drops out

5. Share out the wonderful prize of dead batteries

BUSTED!

What's Behind the Advent-calendar Door?

Santa's Spam pram

Finish It Off

This turkey is off out on the town. Draw it a lovely outfit and colour it in!

What do grumpy mice send each other at Christmas?
Cross-mouse cards

What do reindeer
have that no other
animal has?
Baby reindeer

How do you know
if there's a
reindeer in your
fridge?
*Look for hoof
prints in the
butter*

DICK AND DOM'S CHRISTMAS STUFF
WITH NUTS AND STUFFING

Before snow was invented people used to paint everything white in winter

Christmas used to be in the summer but it got moved as it was parked illegally

Happy Christmas!

At Christmas time in the olden days, the tallest member of the family was thrown down the stairs

Before TV was invented, the queen had to visit every house in the country to do her speech

Christmas
Christmas
Blah Blah
New Year
Blah Blah.
Bye bye.
Woooooo!

26

In Canada they don't send Christmas cards – they send tongue selfies

127

Who is Father
Christmas's most
famous elf?
Elfvis

How do Eskimos
make their beds?
*With sheets of ice
and beds of snow!*

What is a female
elf called?
A shelf

Dick: Can I have a wombat for Christmas?
Dom: *What would you do with a wombat?*
Dick: Play wom of course!

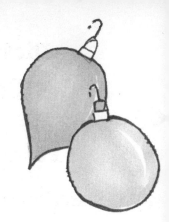

What did the dog get for Christmas?
A mobile bone

Dick and Dom's
Top Five
Things to Leave Out for Father Christmas

1) Ed Sheeran's empty egg box

2) The back end of a boat

3) A stuffed dog in a box

4) Your jam-smeared cousins

5) Seven nights all-inclusive to Crete (£369 per person)

Why did Santa tell off
one of his elves?
*Because he was goblin
his Christmas dinner*

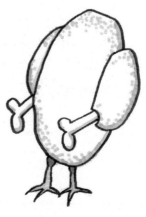

What's the best thing
to put into a Christmas
pudding?
Your teeth!

We had Grandma for Christmas
dinner this year!
Really? We had turkey

What's Behind the Advent-calendar Door?

Rudolph the red-nosed skunk pig

What's the difference between
a reindeer and a biscuit?
*You can't dunk a reindeer in
your tea*

Regular biscuit

Show off!

Christmas cookie

What is Rudolph's
favourite day of
the year?
Red Nose Day

Dick: How was your week skiing, Dom?
Dom: *Interesting. I spent one day skiing and the other six in hospital.*

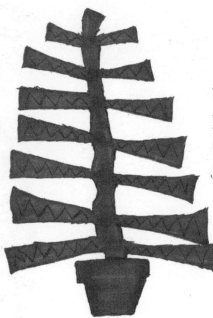

What do vampires put on their turkey at Christmas?
Grave-y

Dick and Dom's
TWELVE DAYS OF CHRISTMAS

On the sixth day of Christmas my Dickie gave to me . . . six greasy doorknobs, five cold things, four pregnant men, three French pigs, two turtles' heads and a fat trout in me mum's tea

How do you tell the difference between a turkey and a carton of custard?

Look at the label

Dom: This turkey tastes like an old sofa!
Dick: *Well, you asked for something with plenty of stuffing.*

Dick: I'm starving. Will the turkey be long?
Dom: *I think it's just going to be turkey-shaped.*

Christmas Wordsearch 2

E	G	G	Y	A	M	P	M	R	S	C	L	A	U	S
L	F	V	U	T	I	O	B	U	T	T	Z	N	H	G
F	A	T	M	W	N	R	J	D	P	Y	M	B	M	I
I	J	E	M	J	C	M	D	O	N	N	E	R	I	N
E	F	N	Y	J	E	E	H	L	O	D	X	C	S	G
S	R	F	K	S	P	A	M	P	R	A	M	S	T	E
T	T	A	A	A	I	T	D	H	R	Y	A	D	L	R
I	K	I	D	U	E	W	A	Q	E	P	S	F	E	B
C	H	R	I	S	T	M	A	S	T	R	E	E	T	R
K	U	Y	G	A	M	Q	V	J	A	E	S	G	O	E
S	M	L	T	G	M	O	U	S	E	S	J	H	E	A
P	B	I	U	E	R	E	I	N	D	E	E	R	R	D
R	U	G	X	S	X	F	J	F	H	N	K	R	D	R
O	G	H	K	Z	N	V	O	M	I	T	I	N	G	C
U	T	T	O	I	L	E	T	A	C	S	E	W	U	C
T	J	S	B	R	A	N	D	Y	B	U	T	T	E	F

Words run down and left to right.

BRANDY BUTTER

BUTT

CHRISTMAS TREE

DONNER

EGGY

ELFIE STICK

FAIRY LIGHTS

FAT

GINGERBREAD

HUMBUG

MEAT

MINCE PIE

MISTLETOE

MOUSE

MRS CLAUS

PRESENTS

REINDEER

RUDOLPH

SAUSAGES

SPAM PRAM

SPROUT

TOILET

VOMITING

XMAS

YUMMY

What is white,
lives at the North
Pole and runs
around naked?
A polar bare!

Why don't penguins fly?
Because they can't reach the controls

What do
sheep
say at
Christmas?
*'Season's
bleatings!'*

Who delivers Christmas
presents to pets?
Santa paws

What's red, white and bouncy?
Santa on a pogo stick!

What two things should you never eat before breakfast on Christmas Day?
Lunch and dinner

What did the
reindeer say
to the elf?
*Nothing – reindeer
can't talk!*

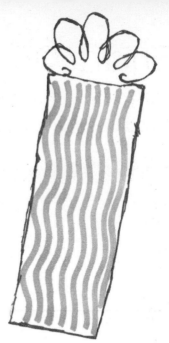

Which reindeer can
jump higher than
a house?
*All of them. Houses
can't jump!*

Finish It Off

Finish this drawing of a Christmas tree decorated with delicious meat products.

**Why did the turkey
join the band?**
*Because it had the
drumsticks*

**What do you get if
you cross a shark
with a snowman?**
Frostbite

Dick: Where does your
auntie come from?
Dom: *Alaska*.
Dick: Don't worry, I'll
ask her myself.

What's
Behind the
Advent-
calendar
Door?

Knickerbocker-
knickers

What happens
if you eat
the Christmas
decorations?
You get tinsellitis

What goes, 'Now you
see me, now you don't,
now you see me, now
you don't'?
*A snowman walking
over a zebra crossing*

Dick and Dom's
Top Five
Uses for Eggnog

1) Take it to *Dragon's Den* and ask for £50,000 of investment

2) Tip it over your nan's head

3) Pour it on to a thin tray – freeze it and make a mini egg ice rink for frogs

4) Use it to clean your neighbours' windows, then ask them for money

5) Try to use it as a playdough substitute and make a model of Ben Shephard from the telly

What do you call a
vicar on a scooter?
Rev

What do you call an elf
with a cow on its head?
Pat

What's green, covered
in tinsel and says,
'Ribbit, ribbit'?
Mistle-toad

Where do you find
elves?
*It depends on where
you left them*

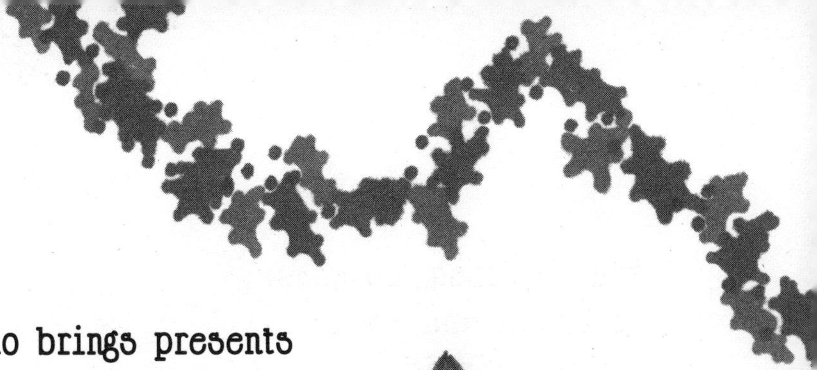

Who brings presents
to baby sharks?
Santa Jaws

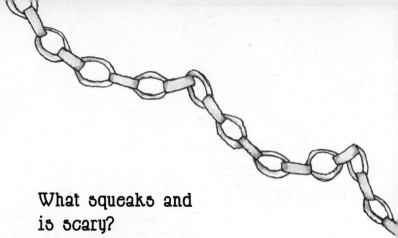

**What squeaks and
is scary?**
*The Ghost of
Christmouse Past*

What kind of bread
do elves use to make
sandwiches?
Shortbread

What happens when
snowmen get dandruff?
They get snowflakes

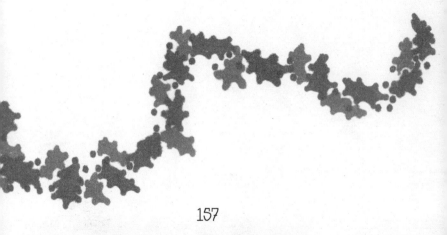

Dick and Dom's
TWELVE DAYS OF CHRISTMAS

On the seventh day of Christmas my Dickie gave to me . . . seven shiny slapheads, six greasy doorknobs, five cold things, four pregnant men, three French pigs, two turtles' heads and a fat trout in me mum's tea

Why didn't Father
Christmas get wet when
he lost his umbrella?
It wasn't raining

What goes,
'Ho, ho, ho, plop, plop, plop!'
Father Christmas on the loo

What do snowmen eat
for lunch?
Icebergers

Why was Santa's little
helper depressed?
He had low elf-esteem

Why do elves scratch themselves?
Because they're the only ones who know where they're itchy!

What medicine does
a snowman take when
he's ill?
A chill pill

What goes, 'Ho, ho, ho,
swoosh, swoosh, swoosh'?
Santa in a revolving door

What's Behind the Advent-calendar Door?

A remote-control bum

What does Tarzan sing
at Christmas time?
'Jungle Bells'

How do you make an
idiot laugh on New
Year's Day?
*Tell him a joke on
Christmas Day*

Where's the best place to put your Christmas tree?
Between your Christmas two and your Christmas four

Dick and Dom's
Top Five
Things to Stuff the Turkey with

1) Some stuff

2) A stuffed cat

3) Stuff and nonsense

4) David Walliams's big flappy hands

5) Stuff this

Which Christmas Carol is popular in the desert?
'*O Camel Ye Faithful*'

Elf Dom: Rudolph just swallowed my pencil, what should I do?
Father Christmas: *Use a pen.*

What do you call
an elf who likes
to dunk biscuits
in his tea?
Duncan

What kind of
bills do elves
have to pay?
Jingle bills

What did the
police officer say
when he saw the
snowman stealing
something?
'Freeze!'

What do snowmen
love to drink?
Iced tea

What did the elf
say when he was
teaching Santa to
use a computer?
'First, yule log in.'

What did the snowman's wife give
him when she was angry with him?
The cold shoulder

Christmas Crossword 2

* see page 217 for a clue!
** see page 13 for a clue!

Across

1) Something you hang at the end of your bed for Santa to put presents in (8)

4) A fun theatre show with lots of boos and hissing (5)

5) You can have either sprouts _ _ cabbage (2)

6) Many carols can be improved by adding the words, 'fudge _ _ _ _ _ _' (6)*

8) If you slip on ice, you'll probably land on your _ _ _ (3)

9) On the fifth day of Christmas, my true love gave to me, five gold _ _ _ _ _ (5)

11) A festive game of ping-pong is rubbish if you only have balls and no _ _ _ _ (4)

12) A yucky yellow drink that grown-ups like is called egg_ _ _ (3)

13) When carollers come round, they always ring the door_ _ _ _ (4)

Down

1) Who hides in the bakery at Christmas? *A mince* _ _ _ (3)**

2) To get to the paper hats, you have to pull your Christmas _ _ _ _ _ _ _ _ (8)

3) On the twelfth day of Christmas, my true love gave to me, twelve drummers _ _ _ _ _ _ _ _ (8)

6) You'd hang this glass ornament on the Christmas tree (6)

7) You can wrap this shiny stuff around anything you like to make it Christmassy (6)

10) 'Carol' is just a fancy word for '_ _ _ _' (4)

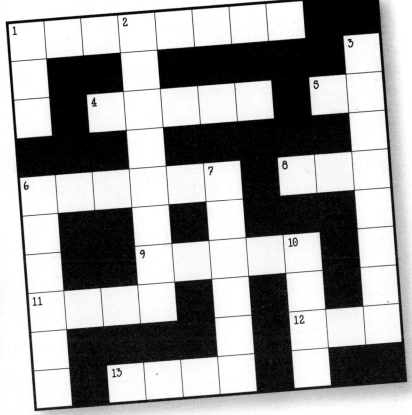

What does Father
Christmas use when he
goes fishing?
His North Pole

What do you get when
you cross a snowman
with a polar bear?
A brrrr-grrrr

What do you call a penguin
in the Sahara desert?
Lost

How do cats greet each other at Christmas?
'*A furry merry Christmas and a happy mew year.*'

Real trees

I ♥ XMAS

KING KONG MERRILY ON HIGH ♪

What is a monkey's favourite Christmas carol?
'*King Kong Merrily on High*'

A Letter to Father Christmas

Dear Santa,

Let's banter! This Christmas I've thought long and hard so here's my list. I want:

World Peace
No Wars
Happiness for everyone
General Positivity everywhere

You see, gifts are great, but if everyone in the world just got together and er . . . oh . . . forget it . . . sack it all off, chubby cheeks!
Just get me a remote-controlled car and a packet of Wagon Wheels.

Epic bants,
Freddie

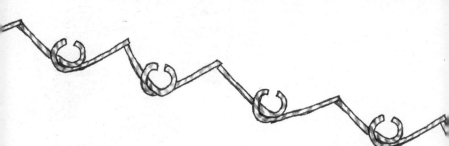

Dick: Doctor, doctor, Father Christmas gives me an orange every year. Now I think I'm turning into one!

Doctor: *Have you tried playing squash?*

Knock, knock!
Who's there?
Mary.
Mary who?
Mary Christmas!

What do you have in December that you don't have in any other month?
The letter 'D'

Why do penguins carry fish in their beaks?
Because they don't have any pockets

What kind of motorbike
does Santa ride?
A Holly-Davidson

What do you call an
old snowman?
Water

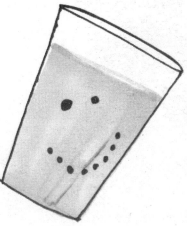

What's Behind the Advent-calendar Door?

Inflatable Bethlehem

Dick and Dom's
Top Five
Things to Hang on Your Tree

1) Scotch-egg balls

2) Cheese balls

3) Falafel balls

4) Lottery balls

5) Ed Balls
   (Former MP)

How do you scare a snowman?
With a hairdryer

What happens
if you're naughty
before Christmas?
*You won't get any
presents and yule
be sorry!*

What are red and green
and grow on the ocean
floor?
Christmas corals

Dom: Waiter, waiter, my Christmas pudding is off!
Waiter: *Off? Where to?*

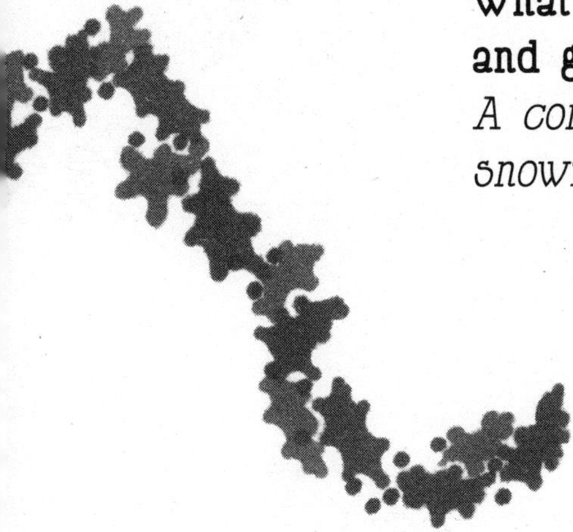

What is white
and goes up?
*A confused
snowflake*

What comes at the end
of Christmas Day?
'Y'

Dick and Dom's
TWELVE DAYS OF CHRISTMAS

On the eighth day of Christmas my Dickie
gave to me . . . eight dogs a-blowing,
seven shiny slapheads, six greasy
doorknobs, five cold things, four pregnant
men, three French pigs, two turtles' heads
and a fat trout in me mum's tea

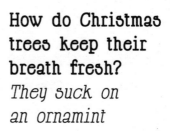

How do Christmas trees keep their breath fresh?
They suck on an ornamint

Did you hear about the Christmas crackers' party?
It went with a bang

Dom: Good news and bad news, Dick – my aunt just gave me a goldfish for Christmas.
Dick: *So what's the bad news?*
Dom: I get the bowl next Christmas . . .

What's the best Christmas gift for someone who likes to play it cool?
A fridge-stereo

Dick: Do you remember
that plate you gave me last
Christmas and you were
worried I might break it?
Dom: *Yes.*
Dick: Well . . . your
worries are over!

Dick and Dom's
Top Five
Reindeer Names

1) Dangle Chops

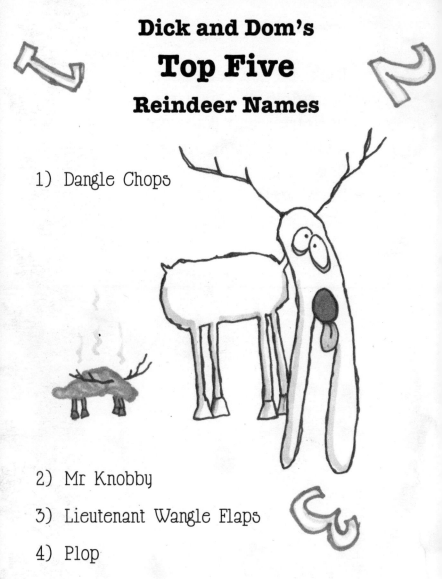

2) Mr Knobby

3) Lieutenant Wangle Flaps

4) Plop

5) Great-Uncle Earnest Godfrey Piggot-Smith

What's
Behind the
Advent-
calendar
Door?

Half a
hairy Twix

Dick: I'm trying to buy a present for my mate Dom. Can you help me out?
Shop assistant: *Certainly, sir. Which way did you come in?*

What's red and white and goes round and round?
Santa in a washing machine

Why should you never invite a footballer to Christmas dinner?

Because he won't stop dribbling

Finish It Off

Finish this drawing of a snowman with his melted friend and colour it in!

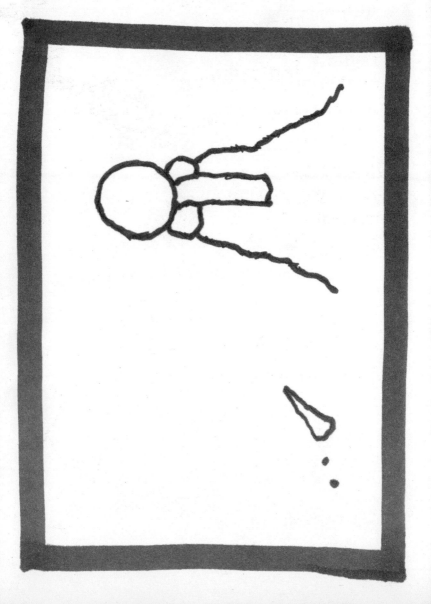

What did the bald
man say when he
got a comb for
Christmas?
*'Thanks, I'll never
part with it.'*

What do snowmen
like to put on their
icebergers?
Chilly sauce

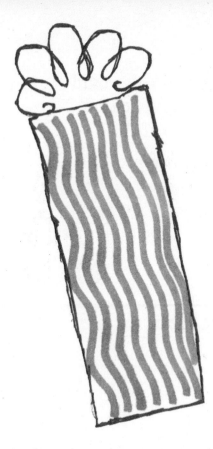

What's the wettest animal
in the world?
A rain-deer

What did one candle
say to the other?
*'Are you going out
tonight?'*

How did Rudolph
learn to read?
He was elf-taught

Where does Santa stay
when he's on holiday?
In a ho, ho, hotel!

Knock, knock!
Who's there?
Wenceslas.
Wenceslas who?
Wenceslas bus
home on Christmas
Eve?

How do whales carry
their Christmas presents?
In a whale-barrow!

Festive

BOREDOM BUSTERS

The World's Finest Stinking Fart Cannon

1) Go to your local *Skunks R Us* store and buy the finest big fat stinking skunk* you can afford

2) Go to *Bagpipes R Us* and buy some floppy bagpipes

3) Attach the bagpipes to the skunk's bum using sticky tape

4) Encourage the skunk to eat lots of lovely sprouts

5) Wait until the skunk starts chuffing and enjoy the Christmas songs your skunk will fart out

Happy stinking Christmas!

*Don't actually do this – skunks have feelings too!

BUSTED!

Dom: Waiter, waiter, my turkey has gone off!
Waiter: *Which way did it go?*

Why do elves wear running shoes?
For running, of course!

Where was Santa
when the lights
went out?
In the dark

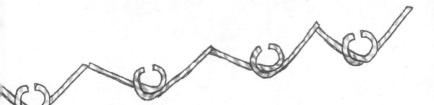

What happened
when Santa's dog
ate garlic?
*His bark was worse
than his bite*

What happened when Mrs Christmas
served soap flakes instead of
cornflakes for breakfast?
*Father Christmas was so angry he
foamed at the mouth*

What kind of coat
does Santa wear when
it rains on Christmas
Eve?
A wet one

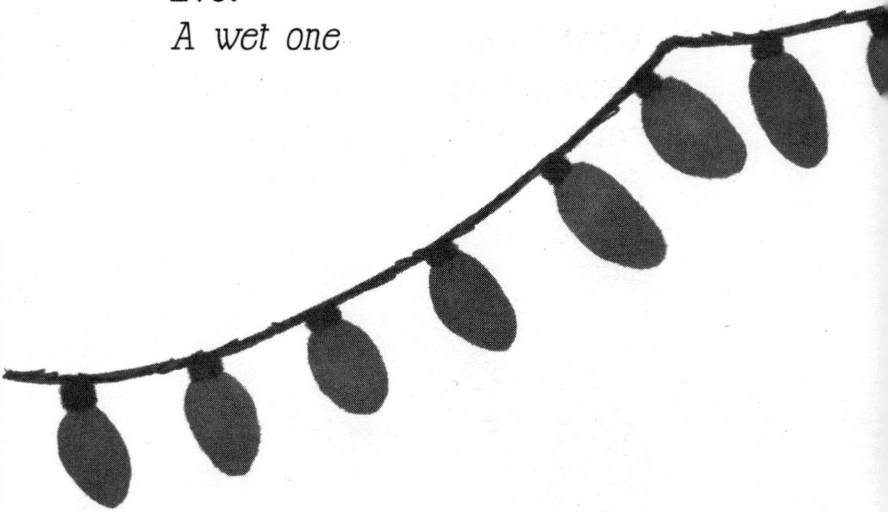

Father Christmas: Elf
Dom, call me a taxi!
Elf Dom: *You're a taxi!*

What's the difference between a reindeer and a snowball?
They're both brown, except the snowball

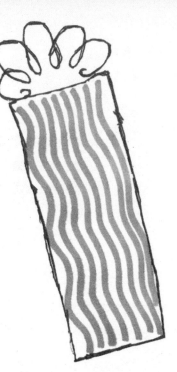

How do you get milk from a polar bear?
Rob its fridge and run like mad!

What's Behind the Advent-calendar Door?

A badly drawn lady

Finish It Off

Finish this drawing of something completely random exploding out of a cracker!

What do you call
a cow at the
North Pole?
An eski-moo

What do elves
use for making
Christmas cakes?
Elf-raising flour

Dom: Doctor, doctor, I keep imagining I'm a snow-covered field.
Doctor: *What's come over you?*
Dom: Two sleighs, three polar bears and a flock of penguins.

What's a turkey's favourite kind of TV show?
A duck-umentary

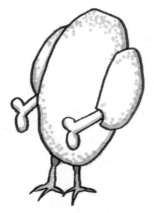

Dick: Did you hear about the stupid turkey?
Dom: *Why was it so stupid?*
Dick: It was looking forward to Christmas.

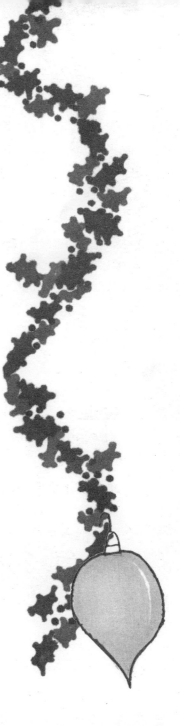

Dick and Dom's
TWELVE DAYS OF CHRISTMAS

On the ninth day of Christmas my Dickie
gave to me . . . nine babies vomming,
eight dogs a-blowing, seven shiny
slapheads, six greasy doorknobs, five
cold things, four pregnant men, three
French pigs, two turtles' heads and a fat
trout in me mum's tea

Knock, knock!
Who's there?
Carol singers.
Do you know what flipping time of night it is?
No, but if you hum it, we'll sing it!

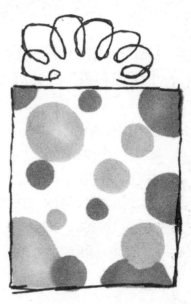

What did one Christmas tree say to the other?
'I've got a present fir you!'

What kind of key
is the best to get
at Christmas?
A monkey

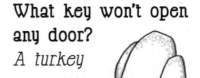

What key won't open
any door?
A turkey

Dick and Dom's
Top Five

Christmas Songs (that are improved
by adding the words 'fudge bucket')

1) 'We Wish You a Merry Fudge Bucket'

2) 'Do They Know it's Fudge-Bucket Time'

3) 'I Wish it Could Be Fudge Bucket Every Day'

4) 'Fudge Bucket is Coming to Town'

5) 'Fairytale of New Fudge Bucket'

Why didn't the elf get any sleep?
He plugged his electric blanket into the toaster by mistake – and kept popping out of bed all night

Dom: Would you like a pocket calculator for Christmas, Dick?
Dick: *No, thanks. I already know how many pockets I have.*

What do you call a
reindeer with a number
plate on its rump?
Reg

Why do reindeer
have fur coats?
*Because they'd look
silly in polyester*

How do you know when there is a snowman in your bed?
You wake up wet

What is Father Christmas's wife called?
Joan

THIS IS MY WIFE. SHE'S CALLED JOAN. JOAN CHRISTMAS.

DICK AND DOM'S CHRISTMAS STUFF
WITH NUTS AND STUFFING

If you keep chestnuts in the fire for too long they fudge up your chimney

David Cameron saves money by wrapping his presents in bacon

from Davcam

If all the power used for Christmas lights was saved up – you could boil four kettles

The French translation of
'Ho ho ho!' is 'Le ho ho ho!'

Mariah Carey's song
'All I Want for
Christmas Is You' is to
be renamed 'All I Want
for Christmas Is Fruit
Shoots'

How did Darth Vader know
what Luke Skywalker had
for Christmas?
He felt his presents

Knock, knock!
Who's there?
Doughnut.
Doughnut who?
Doughnut open until Christmas Day!

STOP ... CAROL TIME

Fill in the blanks to make up new versions of famous carols using the list of words below.

HAMSTER JAM

FISH FINGER

DICK AND DOM

SLUG STUFF

ANGRY TOILET

OWL GAS

SILLY SHIH-TZU

BRIAN

Dashing through the _____,

In a one-horse open _____,

O'er the fields we go,

_____ all the way.

Bells on bobtail _____,

Making spirits bright,

What fun it is to laugh and _____

A sleighing song tonight!

Jingle _____, jingle _____,

Jingle all the way!

Oh, what fun it is to _____

In a one-horse open sleigh!

What's the most popular wine at Christmas?

'*Do I have to eat those Brussels sprouts?*'

Who beats his chest
and swings from
Christmas cake to
Christmas cake?
Tarzipan

What kind of
bird can write?
A PENguin

Why do birds fly south in winter?
Because it's too far to walk

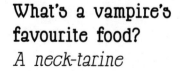

What's a vampire's favourite food?
A neck-tarine

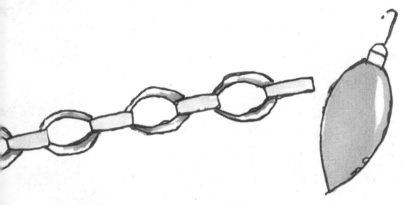

What's Behind the Advent-calendar Door?

Mary Berry
up a
flagpole

Dick and Dom's
TWELVE DAYS OF CHRISTMAS

On the tenth day of Christmas my Dickie
gave to me . . . ten boils a-seeping, nine
babies vomming, eight dogs a-blowing,
seven shiny slapheads, six greasy
doorknobs, five cold things, four pregnant
men, three French pigs, two turtles' heads
and a fat trout in me mum's tea

What don't you want to find in your stocking at Christmas?
A massive hole

What do skunks sing at Christmas?
'Jingle Smells'

What do DJs love about
Christmas?
All the rapping

Why do snowmen live
out in the snow?
Because it's cool!

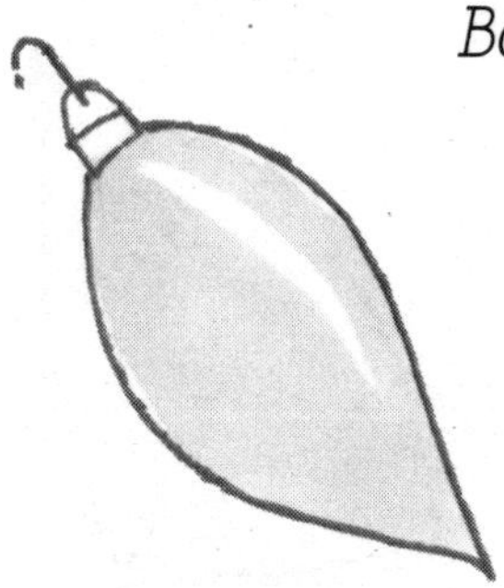

Why did Father Christmas get a parking ticket?
He left his sleigh in a 'snow parking' zone

What's Behind the Advent-calendar Door?

Mongoose juice

How many presents
can Santa fit in an
empty sack?
*Just the one. After
that the sack's not
empty any more*

What do reindeer
hang on their
Christmas trees?
Hornaments

Why is Rudolph so
good at quizzes?
Because he nose a lot

What did the
penguin say when
it swam into
a wall?
'Dam!'

Why did the elf
refuse to get
married in
an igloo?
She got cold feet

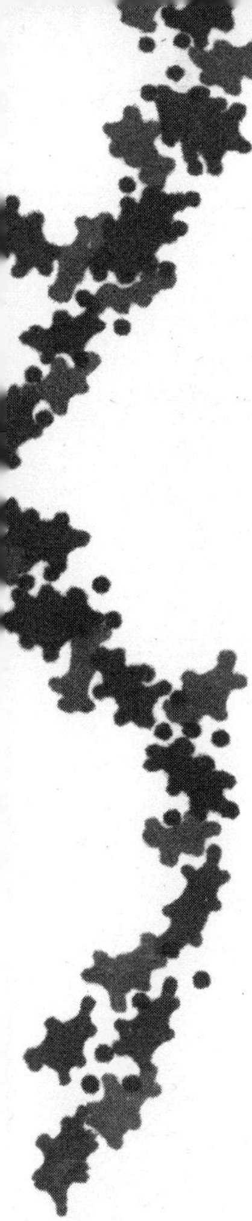

Why did the
Christmas cake go
to the doctor?
*He was feeling
crummy*

How do you make
opening your
presents last
longer?
*Open them with
boxing gloves on*

What did the
custard say to
the jelly?
*"Tis the season to
be jelly . . ."*

241

A Letter to Father Christmas

Dear Mr Christmas,

Last year you gave my son Little Willy a book called *Dick and Dom's Whoopee Book of Practical Jokes*. As a result of this, I have been pranked all year. Not a day goes by when I don't have fake dog poo in my breakfast, get woken up at 3 a.m. by all the alarms in the house, put salt in my tea instead of sugar or all kinds of other pranks that generally mess with my noodle.

Please don't bother stopping here this year, unless you can actually bring Dick and Dom in person so I can give their hair a nice wash in our toilet, then throw them in the basement for a few hours.

Thanks for your time. Sincerely,
Willy Senior
Father of Little Willy (Junior)

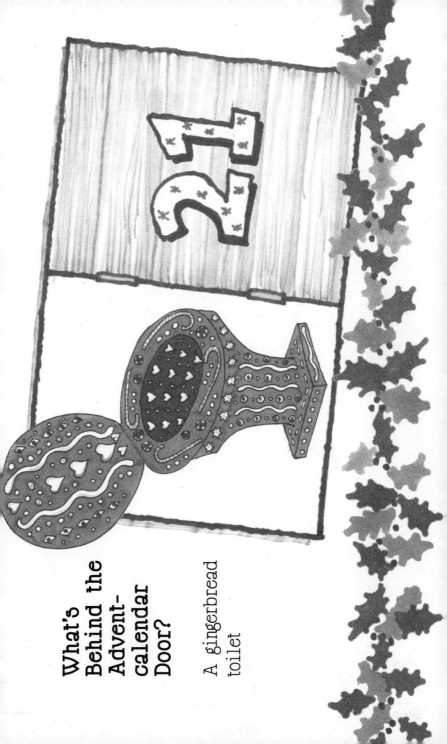

What's
Behind the
Advent-
calendar
Door?

A gingerbread
toilet

What is six metres
tall, has sharp
teeth and says,
'Ho, ho, ho!'?
Tyranno-santa rex

Who carries all
Father Christmas's books?
His book elf

What's the most boring animal?
A polar bore

How do snowmen get around?
On ice-icles

What did the cow say on Christmas morning?
'Mooey Christmas!'

What do you get if you cross a centipede with a turkey?
Drumsticks for everyone!

Why is it so hard to keep a secret in the North Pole?
Because your teeth chatter

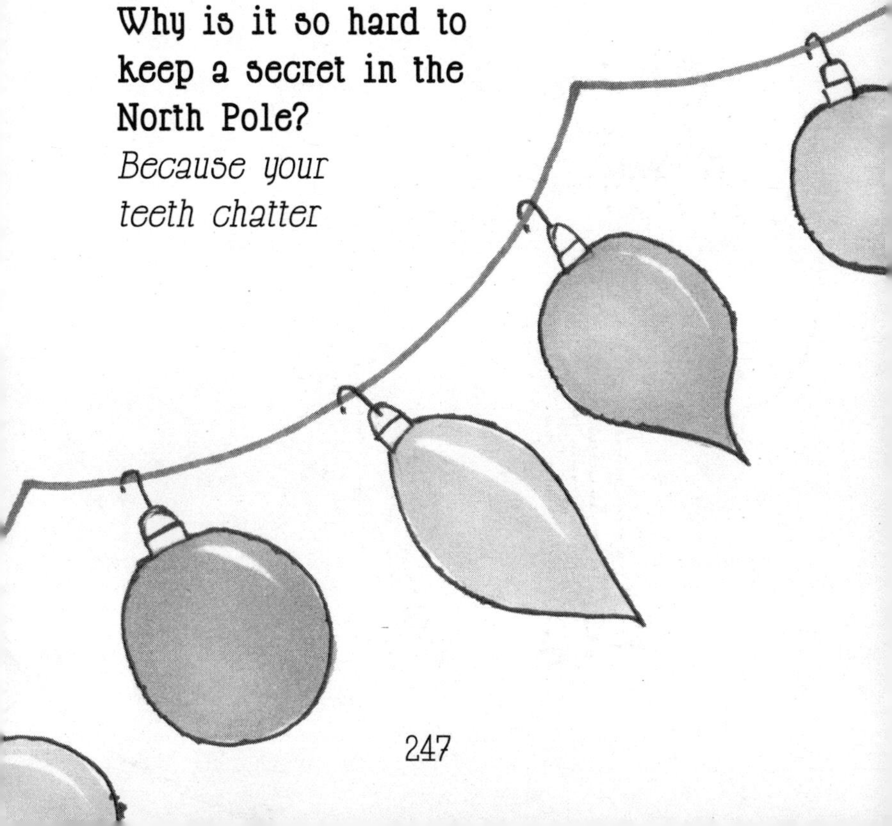

Christmas Join the Dots 2

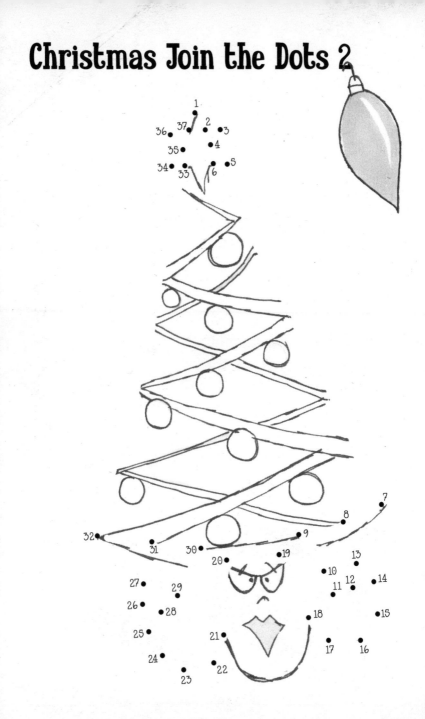

249

See pages 294–295
for answers

What happened to the man who stole a calendar?

He got twelve months

What does the Queen call her Christmas broadcast?

The One Show!

Finish It Off

Finish this drawing of the contents of Father Christmas's hanky and colour it in.

What's
Behind the
Advent-
calendar
Door?

A bungee-
jumping
choirboy

Which side of a
penguin has the
most feathers?
The outside!

How does a penguin
build a house?
Igloos it together

What is brown,
has a hump and
lives at the
South Pole?
A very lost camel

What do you get
when you cross a
snowman with a
vampire?
Frostbite

What athlete is
warmest in winter?
A long jumper!

How do you know if Santa
is really a werewolf?
He has Santa claws

Make Your Own Snow Globe

1) Get an empty jam jar

2) Get the hairy kid from down the street and ask him to shake his dandruff into the jar

3) Mix some water with toothpaste, grit and cockle juice and pour into jar with the dandruff

4) Mould a piece of corned beef into the shape of your sleeping grandad and glue it to the lid of the jar

5) Put the lid on, shake it about and watch the magical Christmas scene inside come alive

6)

Vomit!

BUSTED!

What did the
stamp say to the
Christmas card?
*'Stick with me and
we'll go places!'*

Why is it getting harder to buy
Advent calendars?
Because their days are numbered

What kind of maths do snowy owls like?
Owlgebra

Dick and Dom's
Top Five

Pantos (that are improved by adding the words 'dog poo')

1) *Dog Poos in the Wood*

2) *Snow White and the Seven Dog Poos*

3) *Beauty and the Dog Poo*

4) *Mother Dog Poo*

5) *Puss in Dog Poo*

What's Behind the Advent-calendar Door?

Little donkey's little brother

*Actual size

Why did the
Brussels sprout
go to jail?
*Because it was a
repeat offender*

Why did no one
bid for Rudolph
and Dasher on
eBay?
*Because they were
two deer*

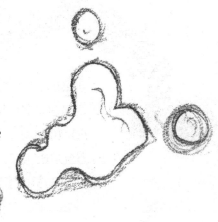

How do you know if
Father Christmas has
been in your shed?
*Because you have
three extra hoes*

MEGA LOLS!

Teacher: If I have twenty pounds and ask Ebenezer Scrooge for another thirty pounds, how much would I have?

Dom: *Twenty pounds.*

Teacher: You don't know your arithmetic!

Dom: *You don't know Scrooge!*

What do the elves sing to Father Christmas on his birthday?

'Freeze a jolly good fellow!'

Dick and Dom's
TWELVE DAYS OF CHRISTMAS

On the eleventh day of Christmas my
Dickie gave to me . . . eleven teeth and
lips, ten boils a-seeping, nine babies
vomming, eight dogs a-blowing, seven
shiny slapheads, six greasy doorknobs,
five cold things, four pregnant men, three
French pigs, two turtles' heads and a fat
trout in me mum's tea

What do you get if you cross an iPad and a Christmas tree?
A pineapple

What's a maths teacher's favourite festive treat?
Mince pi

What's a snowman's favourite lesson at school?
Snow and tell

Dick: What are you going
to give Dave for Christmas
this year?
Dom: *I haven't decided yet.*
Dick: What did you give
him last year?
Dom: *Food poisoning.*

What do you call
Santa Claus when he
doesn't move?
Santa Pause!

What do you call an
elf that slides around
on a piece of toast?
Marge

Dick and Dom's
Top Five

Carols (that are improved by adding the words 'bum chutney')

1) 'O Little Town of Bum Chutney'

2) 'Ding Dong Merrily on Bum Chutney'

3) 'O Come, All Ye Bum Chutney'

4) 'Once in Royal David's Bum Chutney'

5) 'While Shepherds Watched Their Bum Chutney'

What's Behind the Advent-calendar Door?

The Christmas-pudding-headed boy

Why are turkeys wiser than chickens?
Have you ever heard of Kentucky Fried Turkey?

NOW THAT LOOKS REEAAAL APPETIZIN'

What's the best thing to give your parents for Christmas? *A list of everything you want!*

What do you call a snowman with a six-pack? *The abdominal snowman*

Did you hear about the cat that swallowed Mrs Christmas's knitting?
She had mittens

Dom: I told Father Christmas you were good this year . . .
Dick: *And?*
Dom: He hasn't stopped laughing since.

Finish It Off

Finish this drawing of an evil Christmas pudding and colour it in!

DICK AND DOM'S CHRISTMAS STUFF
WITH NUTS AND STUFFING

After Christmas, Lapland
becomes Poundland

Rudolph's red nose is
actually brown, but it's
very, very angry

Sprouts are actually made in a skunk-powered fart tunnel

If you light your fire on Christmas Eve, Father Christmas gets to piddle down the chimney

Father Christmas's favourite nuts are chestnuts, walnuts, hazelnuts and chuff nuts

Where do seals go to
watch Christmas movies?
To the dive-in!

Knock, knock!
Who's there?
Arthur.
Arthur who?
Arthur any
mince pies
left?

278

Dick and Dom's
TWELVE DAYS OF CHRISTMAS

On the twelfth
day of
Christmas my
Dickie gave to
me . . . twelve
hippies' fingers,
eleven teeth
and lips, ten
boils a-seeping,
nine babies
vomming, eight
dogs a-blowing, seven shiny slapheads,
six greasy doorknobs, five cold things,
four pregnant men, three French pigs,

two turtles'
heads and a
fat trout in
me mum's tea

What do you call
a prawn that won't
share its Christmas
presents?
Shell-fish

Dom: I got my wife a
wooden leg for Christmas?
Dick: *Oh yeah?*
Dom: It's not her main
present – just a stocking
filler.

What's the difference
between an iceberg and a
clothes brush?
*One crushes boats and the
other brushes coats!*

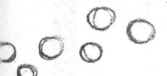

Why don't aliens
celebrate Christmas?
*Because they don't want
to give away
their presence*

What did the snowman
say to the aggressive
carrot?
'Get out of my face!'

Finish It Off

Finish this drawing of a snotty five-eyed, eight-legged choirboy eating sprouts.

How do Christmas
trees get online?
They log in

What kind of clothes
do baby reindeers
wear?
Hoof-me-downs

What do you get
if you cross Santa
with a duck?
*A Christmas
quacker*

If the sun shines while it's snowing, what should you look for?
Snowbows!

What did the sea say to Father Christmas?
Nothing, it just waved!

What's Behind the Advent-calendar Door?

Edward
Christmas-
candle-
fingers

Solution to Christmas Wordsearch 1

Pages 54–55

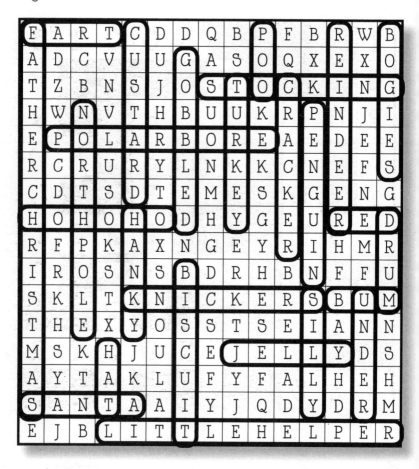

Solution to Christmas Crossword 1

Pages 88–89

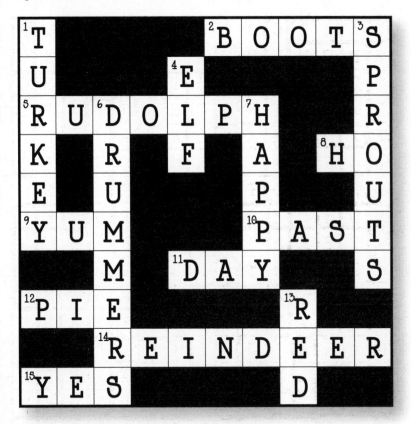

Solutions to Christmas Join the Dots 1

Pages 114–115

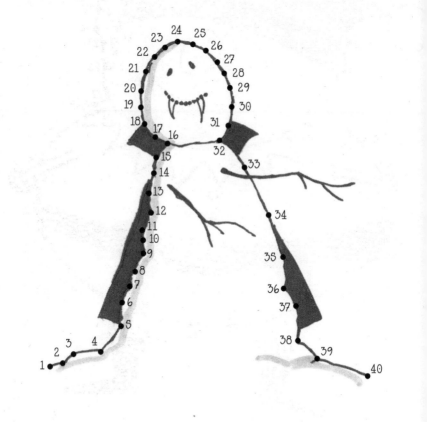

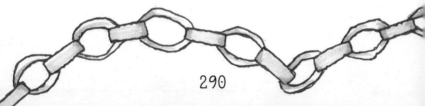

Solution to Christmas Wordsearch 2

Pages 140–141

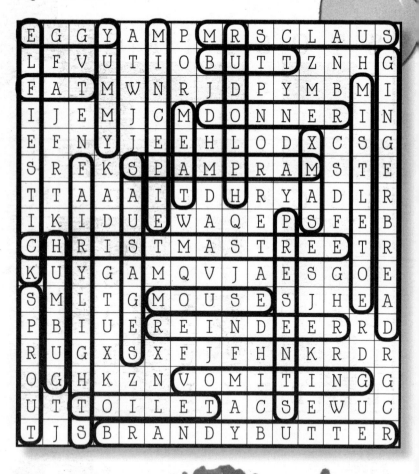

E	G	G	Y	A	M	P	M	R	S	C	L	A	U	S
L	F	V	U	T	I	O	B	U	T	T	Z	N	H	G
F	A	T	M	W	N	R	J	D	P	Y	M	B	M	I
I	J	E	M	J	C	M	D	O	N	N	E	R	I	N
E	F	N	Y	J	E	E	H	L	O	D	X	C	S	G
S	R	F	K	S	P	A	M	P	R	A	M	S	T	E
T	T	A	A	I	T	D	H	R	Y	A	D	L	E	R
I	K	I	D	U	E	W	A	Q	E	P	S	F	E	B
C	H	R	I	S	T	M	A	S	T	R	E	E	T	R
K	U	Y	G	A	M	Q	V	J	A	E	S	G	O	E
S	M	L	T	G	M	O	U	S	E	S	J	H	E	A
P	B	I	U	E	R	E	I	N	D	E	E	R	R	D
R	U	G	X	S	X	F	J	F	H	N	K	R	D	R
O	G	H	K	Z	N	V	O	M	I	T	I	N	G	G
U	T	T	O	I	L	E	T	A	C	S	E	W	U	C
T	J	S	B	R	A	N	D	Y	B	U	T	T	E	R

292

Solution to Christmas Crossword 2

Pages 172–173

¹S	T	O	²C	K	I	N	G		
P			R						³D
Y		⁴P	A	N	T	O		⁵O	R
			C						U
⁶B	U	C	K	E	⁷T		⁸B	U	M
A			E		I				M
U		⁹R	I	N	G	S	¹⁰S		I
¹¹B	A	T	S		S		O		N
L					E		¹²N	O	G
E		¹³B	E	L	L		G		

293

Solutions to Christmas Join the Dots 2

Pages 248–249

Have you read these?

Dick and Dom's
BIG FAT and VERY SILLY
JOKE book

Funny stuff, facts, fibs and chick

Dick and Dom's
WHOOPEE BOOK OF
PRACTICAL JOKES

Also includes titters, nuggets and more stuff what we wrote!

Dick and Dom's
SLIGHTLY NAUGHTY BUT VERY SILLY
WORDS